This
Treasure Cove Story
belongs to

**BABY SHARK AND
THE COLOURS OF THE OCEAN**

A CENTUM BOOK 978-1-913265-84-7
Published in Great Britain by Centum Books Ltd.
This edition published 2020.

3 5 7 9 10 8 6 4 2

Centum Books Ltd, 20 Devon Square, Newton Abbot, Devon, TQ12 2HR, UK.
9/10 Fenian St, Dublin 2, D02 RX24, Ireland.

www.centumbooksltd.co.uk | books@centumbooksltd.co.uk
CENTUM BOOKS Limited Reg.No. 07641486.

A CIP catalogue record for this book is available
from the British Library.

Printed in China.

pinkfong
BABY SHARK™

A Treasure Cove Story

Baby Shark and the Colours of the Ocean

Baby Shark is sat with his big photo
album open in front of him.
Why does his face look so gloomy?
What's wrong, Baby Shark?

'All my photos look dull and grey, the beautiful colours have faded away!' says Baby Shark. Baby Shark's photos are all completely colourless! What should we do, Baby Shark?

'Don't worry,' says Baby Shark. 'I will colour the photos again with my magic crayons! Baby Shark, doo-doo-doo-doo-doo! Colourful marks, doo-doo-doo-doo-doo!'

'Who should I colour with red?'
wonders Baby Shark.

Who are Baby Shark's RED friends who live under the ocean?

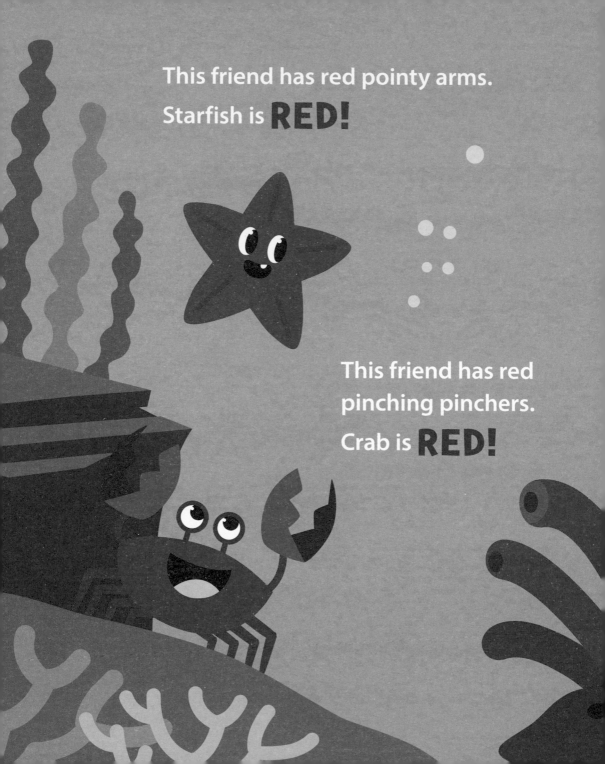

This friend has red pointy arms.
Starfish is **RED!**

This friend has red
pinching pinchers.
Crab is **RED!**

This friend has red
wavy tentacles.

Sea anemone is RED!

'That takes care of all my friends who are red!'
says Baby Shark.

'Who should I colour with green?'
wonders Baby Shark.

Who are Baby Shark's GREEN friends who live under the ocean?

This friend has
a curly green tail.
Seahorse is **GREEN!**

This friend has
green wavy hair.
Wavy seaweed is
GREEN!

This friend has a
tough green shell.

Sea turtle is **GREEN!**

'That takes care of all my friends who are green!' says Baby Shark.

'Who should I colour with blue?'
wonders Baby Shark.

Who are Baby Shark's BLUE friends who live under the ocean?

A whale is
BLUE!

The deep ocean and Daddy Shark
are **BLUE** too!

'That takes care of all my friends who are blue!'
says Baby Shark.

Baby Shark, which colour is next?

'It's yellow, my favourite colour, of course!'

Who are Baby Shark's YELLOW friends who live under the ocean?

These friends have beautiful yellow scales.
Tropical fish are YELLOW!

This friend has a yellow puffy face.
Blowfish is YELLOW!

'That takes care of yellow!'
says Baby Shark.

Not quite, Baby Shark.
There's still someone else who is yellow...

'Oopsie-daisie! I have missed one, and how could I forget? I am **YELLOW** too!'

RED, GREEN, BLUE and YELLOW!

Baby Shark's photo album is colourful once again. Way to go, Baby Shark!

Treasure Cove Stories

Please contact Centum Books
to receive the full list of titles in
the *Treasure Cove Stories* series.
books@centumbooksltd.co.uk

1 Three Little Pigs
2 Snow White and
the Seven Dwarfs
3 The Fox and the Hound
- Hide-and-Seek
4 Dumbo
5 Cinderella
6 Cinderella's Friends
7 Alice in Wonderland
8 Mad Hatter's Tea Party
from Alice in Wonderland
9 Mickey Mouse and
his Spaceship
10 Peter Pan
11 Pinocchio
12 Mickey and the Beanstalk
13 Sleeping Beauty
and the Good Fairies
14 The Lucky Puppy
15 Chicken Little
16 The Incredibles
17 Coco
18 Winnie the Pooh and Tigger
19 The Sword in the Stone
20 Mary Poppins
21 The Jungle Book
22 Aristocats
23 Lady and the Tramp
24 Bambi
25 Bambi - Friends of the Forest
26 Pete's Dragon
27 Beauty and the Beast
- The Teapot's Tale
28 Monsters, Inc.
– M is for Monster
29 Finding Nemo
30 The Incredibles 2
31 The Incredibles
– Jack-Jack Attack
33 Wall-E
34 Up
35 The Princess and the Frog
36 Toy Story – The Pet Problem

39 Spider-Man – Night of the Vulture!
40 Wreck it Ralph
41 Ralph Breaks the Internet
42 The Invincible Iron Man
– Eye of the Dragon
45 Toy Story – A Roaring Adventure
46 Cars – Deputy Mater Saves
the Day!
47 Spider-Man – Trapped by the
Green Goblin
49 Spider-Man – High Voltage!
50 Frozen
51 Cinderella is my Babysitter
52 Beauty and the Beast
- I am the Beast
56 I am a Princess
57 The Big Book of Paw Patrol
58 Paw Patrol
- Adventures with Grandpa!
59 Paw Patrol - Pirate Pups!
60 Trolls
61 Trolls Holiday
63 Zootropolis
64 Ariel is my Babysitter
65 Tiana is my Babysitter
66 Belle is my Babysitter
67 Paw Patrol
- Itty-Bitty Kitty Rescue
68 Moana
70 Guardians of the Galaxy
71 Captain America
- High-Stakes Heist!
72 Ant-Man
73 The Mighty Avengers
74 The Mighty Avengers
- Lights Out!
75 The Incredible Hulk
78 Paw Patrol - All-Star Pups!
80 I am Ariel
82 Jasmine is my Babysitter
87 Beauty and the Beast - I am Belle
88 The Lion Guard
- The Imaginary Okapi
89 Thor - Thunder Strike!
90 Guardians of the Galaxy
- Rocket to the Rescue!
93 Olaf's Frozen Adventure
95 Trolls - Branch's Bunker Birthday

96 Trolls - Poppy's Party
97 The Ugly Duckling
98 Cars - Look Out for Mater!
99 101 Dalmatians
100 The Sorcerer's Apprentice
101 Tangled
102 Avengers
– The Threat of Thanos
105 The Mighty Thor
106 Doctor Strange
107 Captain Marvel
108 The Invincible Iron Man
110 The Big Freeze
111 Ratatouille
112 Aladdin
113 Aladdin - I am the Genie
114 Seven Dwarfs Find a House
115 Toy Story
116 Toy Story 4
117 Paw Patrol - Jurassic Bark!
118 Paw Patrol
- Mighty Pup Power!
121 The Lion King - I am Simba
122 Winnie the Pooh
- The Honey Tree
123 Frozen II
124 Baby Shark and the
Colours of the Ocean
125 Baby Shark and
the Police Sharks!
126 Trolls World Tour
127 I am Elsa
128 I am Anna
129 I am Olaf
130 I am Mulan
131 Sleeping Beauty
132 Onward
133 Paw Patrol
 – Puppy Birthday to You!
134 Black Widow
135 Trolls – Poppy's Big Day!
136 Baby Shark and the Tooth Fairy
137 Baby Shark – Mummy Shark
138 Inside Out
139 The Prince and the Pauper
140 Finding Dory
142 The Lion King
- Simba's Daring Rescue

•Book list may be subject to change. Not all titles are listed.